DRUMMER BOY
OF JOHN JOHN

by **Mark Greenwood** illustrations by **Frané Lessac**

Lee & Low Books Inc. • New York

The sun beat down on the tropical island of Trinidad. In the village of John John, families and friends toiled in teams, sewing beads onto costumes, decorating masks with feathers and shells.

The hum of calypso music floated on the sea breeze. In two weeks it would be Carnival—a time to jump up and celebrate.

"Let's make this de greatest Carnival ever," declared the Roti King. He promised free rotis for the best band in the parade. People often traveled from all over the island for the Roti King's famous folded pancakes filled with chicken and secret herbs and spices.

Winston wished he was in a band. *Carnival jus' ain't right without a roti*, he thought.

On street corners, musicians practiced for the parade of bands. Chac-chac players shook gourds full of seeds.

shoush-shap
shukka-shac
shoush-shap
shukka-shac

The tamboo bamboo band knocked sticks and pounded the ground.

click **clack** click **clack**
rappa-tap rappa-tap

The bottle-and-spoon orchestra tapped out tinkling tones.

jingle jangle tingle tangle

clink clank clunk

Shango drummers struck up a big bass beat.

boom
boody-boom
chucka boom bam

Winston wandered through the village and followed a goat path to the junkyard at the top of the hill. He sat beneath an old mango tree. *Carnival jus' ain't right without a roti*, he thought. *I need a band.*

Winston peeled a mango with his teeth and ate the juicy flesh. Then he hurled the pit into the junkyard. It bounced off a milk can, ricocheted from a biscuit tin, and struck a rusty old paint bucket.

The sounds surprised Winston. He wandered through the junkyard banging on tins and cans, pots and pans. Each metal container produced a different musical sound. Small biscuit tins made high notes.

ping pom

ping pah

ping pom

Big oil cans made low notes.

tom ping

tom pang

Winston hammered the old metal with sticks and stones until clear notes rang out. Each dent and bump changed the pitch of the sound.

be doo
be dom

He drummed on containers of various shapes and sizes.
He made high notes and low notes. Soon Winston could
play a simple tune.

tom ping
tom pah

The chiming and clanging drew Winston's friends out of their homes and into the street.

"What's dat noise?" they asked. Everyone was curious about the sounds coming from high up on the hill.

Winston ran down from the junkyard to greet his friends.

"Follow me," he said, and led them up the goat path. Under the mango tree he paraded before them, drumming a merry melody.

"Winston's drums sound sweeeet!" they cheered.

That day Winston and his friends formed a band. They painted pots and pans, tins and cans in a rainbow of colors. They wrapped rubber from old tires around the ends of their sticks to mellow the tones when they struck their metal drums.

Every day the junkyard band practiced for Carnival—and dreamed
of winning the Roti King's famous folded pancakes filled with chicken
and secret herbs and spices.

On the morning of Carnival, bells and whistles called musicians and dancers to assemble for the parade.

From throughout the village they came, swinging their hips,
chanting and singing, "Paartiee all day. Paartiee all night."

The tamboo bamboo band pounded
thunderous rhythms.

click clack   click clack
rappa-tap   rappa-tap

The chac-chac players rattled
rustling sounds.

shoush-shap
shukka-shac
shoush-shap
shukka-shac

Shango drummers played
big bass beats.

boom boody-boom
chucka boom bam

The bottle-and-spoon orchestra tapped
tinkling tones.

jingle jangle   clink
tingle   clank
    tangle   clunk

Then, with a crashing wave of sound, Winston and his junkyard band came dancing along the roadside.

be doo be dom tom ping

ping pom ping pang boom bam

They beat and pounded and thumped
their rainbow-colored drums.

tom pah

boom bam

The music swept through the village, weaving a spell up one street, then down another. People clapped their hands, stamped their feet, and danced under the limbo pole to the irresistible rhythms of Winston's junkyard band.

Winston and his friends were crowned the best band in the Carnival parade!
That night they were special guests of the Roti King. At his sidewalk shack
they all sipped mango lemonade and feasted on delicious folded pancakes
filled with chicken and secret herbs and spices.
"Roti tonight," Winston sang. "Rotiiis all night!"

Author's Note

This story was inspired by the early life of Winston "Spree" Simon (1927?–1976), a pioneer in the development of the steel drum, or pan. The proud villagers of John John, Trinidad, believe that Winston was the first person to play a tune on the instrument, although he never claimed that distinction.

Winston grew up in a poor district in the East Dry River section of Port of Spain, the capital of Trinidad. His neighborhood was ringed by factories that produced cookies and crackers and other products that were stored in metal containers. At the age of seven, Winston was a drummer boy in a group called the John John Band. The band made noise on the streets during celebrations such as Carnival and Discovery Day. Winston's "drum," a one-note instrument made from discarded junk, added a percussive highlight to a rhythm section made up of older boys who beat and pounded anything on which they could get their hands.

One day while knocking the surface of his instrument with a stone to alter its shape, Winston was intrigued by the tones and pitches that were produced. Curiosity led him to experiment. He cut a handheld pan from a paint can. Dents, made by striking the pan with a stone, pushed the metal upward to form bumps, which Winston tuned to notes that sounded like *pings* and *pongs*. The instrument became known as a ping-pong pan.

By age nine, Winston was playing melodies on his four-note ping-pong pan in various groups that took to the streets with garbage can lids, biscuit tins, paint cans, and other metal containers. The youngsters were known to be highly skilled in "making noise." During Carnival in the years that followed, the streets of John John resonated with clanging rhythms and melodies thumped out on old metal containers.

Carnival celebrations were banned in Trinidad for most of World War II (1939–1945). Winston used the time to practice on an improved nine-note pan. He is remembered for his performance at Carnival in 1946, where he paraded before the governor of Trinidad and other dignitaries playing "God Save the King" and Franz Schubert's "Ave Maria."

Winston was honored by selection into the Trinidad All Stars Percussion Orchestra, which toured London and Paris in 1951, introducing the steel drum to European audiences. His importance to the history of the instrument is immortalized in several calypso songs, most notably Lord Kitchener's "Tribute to Spree Simon." In 1974 Winston received Trinidad and Tobago's Public Service Medal of Merit for his contribution to the development of the steel band. He is also honored by a monument in John John.

Winston "Spree" Simon's early instruments were made from old paint cans and biscuit tins. Today the steel drum is the national instrument of Trinidad and Tobago, and steel drum orchestras symbolize the musical culture of the Caribbean to the world.

Glossary and Pronunciation Guide

Some pronunciations reflect the way words are spoken in Trinidad.
These words are often pronounced differently in other English-speaking areas of the world.

bass beat (bayss beet): low resonant sound played repeatedly to produce a rhythm

biscuit tin (BISS-kit tin): small metal box for storing cookies or crackers

bottle-and-spoon (BOT-uhl-and-spoon): instrument consisting of glass bottles that are filled with water to different levels and struck with a metal spoon to produce tinkling tones

calypso (kuh-LIP-soh): style of Caribbean music with a strong rhythm

Caribbean (ka-ruh-BEE-uhn *or* kuh-RIB-ee-uhn): of or relating to the Caribbean Sea or its islands, or to the people of the islands

Carnival (kah-nee-VAAL): season immediately before Lent; in Trinidad, a five-day celebration with calypso contests, steel drum band competitions, parties, and dancing in the streets

chac-chac (shak-shak): rattle made from a hollow gourd filled with hard, dried seeds

dat (daht): Trinidadian pronunciation of *that*

de (dee): Trinidadian pronunciation of *the*

gourd (gord): fruit with a hard shell that is used for decoration and to make bowls, containers, and instruments

John John (jon jon): village in the East Dry River section of the capital city of Port of Spain, Trinidad

limbo (LIM-boh): dance or contest in which a person bends backward and moves under a horizontal pole that is lowered slightly after each pass

melody (MEL-uh-dee): sequence of musical notes that creates a tune

note (noht): single musical sound

paartiee (paah-tee): Trinidadian slang for *party*

pitch (pich): highness or lowness of a musical sound

rhythm (RITH-uhm): strong, regular, repeated beat or pattern in music

roti (roh-tee): thin pancake or flatbread; in Trinidad it is fried and then folded around a filling of curried chicken, meat, or fish plus potatoes, onions, tomatoes, herbs, and spices

Shango drum (shang-GOH druhm): hollow wood cylinder with one or two ends covered by animal skin that is tapped with the hands; adds an element of African music to a steel drum orchestra

steel drum (steel druhm): musical instrument developed in Trinidad made from the bottom of an oil barrel that is played by striking raised and tuned portions of the surface; also known as a steel pan

tamboo bamboo (tam-boo bam-boo): band in which players knock together different lengths and thicknesses of bamboo and pound them on the ground to produce percussive rhythms

tone (tohn): difference in pitch between two musical notes

tune (toon): series of musical notes arranged in a pattern

Trinidad (trin-ih-daad): island in the Caribbean off the northeastern coast of Venezuela; part of the country of Trinidad and Tobago

For Marcia—m.g.   For my brother, Michael—f.l.

Author's Sources

Anthony, Michael. "People of the Century, Part One: Birth of Two Pan Pioneers: Ellie Mannette and Winston Simon." *Express*, sec. 2, October 25, 2000: 2–3.

Broughton, Simon, et. al., eds. *World Music: The Rough Guide*. London: Rough Guides/Penguin Books, 1994.

Emrit, Ronald C. "Winston Simon." http://www.bestoftrinidad.com/steelband/simon.html.

Granger, Lynn. "Carnival History Notebook." *Boston Carnival Magazine*, 1999. http://www.bostoncarnival.com/carnival_history.htm.

Hart, Mickey, and Fredric Lieberman. *Planet Drum: A Celebration of Percussion and Rhythm*. New York: HarperCollins, 1991.

Jones, Anthony M. *Steelband: A History*. Port of Spain, Trinidad: Educo Press, 1975.

Mangurian, David. "A short history of the shiny drum." IDB América, June 2001. http://www.iadb.org/idbamerica/English/MAY01e2.html.

Sarina. "Trinidadian Roti—An Overview." Trinigourmet.com. December 13, 2006. http://www.trinigourmet.com/index.php/trinidadian-roti-an-overview/.

Seeger, Peter. *Steel Drums: How to Play and Make Them*. New York: Oak Publications, 1964.

Steel Island. http://www.steelisland.com/history.asp.

"Steel Pans—20th Century Percussion." BBC Home, November 5, 2003. http://www.bbc.co.uk/dna/h2g2/A1297721.

Stuempfle, Stephen. *The Steelband Movement: The Forging of a National Art in Trinidad and Tobago*. Philadelphia: University of Pennsylvania Press, 1995.

Wu, Corinna. "Musical Metal." *Science News*. October 10, 1998: 236–238.

Text copyright © 2012 by Mark Greenwood   Illustrations copyright © 2012 by Frané Lessac

All rights reserved. No part of this book may be reproduced, transmitted, or stored in an information retrieval system in any form or by any means, electronic, mechanical, photocopying, recording, or otherwise, without written permission from the publisher.

LEE & LOW BOOKS Inc., 95 Madison Avenue, New York, NY 10016

leeandlow.com

Book design by Scott Myles Studios   Book production by The Kids at Our House

The text is set in Jacoby   The illustrations are rendered in gouache

Manufactured in China by Jade Productions, June 2012

10 9 8 7 6 5 4 3 2 1

First Edition

Library of Congress Cataloging-in-Publication Data

Greenwood, Mark.

    Drummer boy of John John / by Mark Greenwood ; illustrations by Frané Lessac. — 1st ed.

      p. cm.

    Summary: "A story inspired by events in the boyhood of Winston 'Spree' Simon, a pioneer in the development of the steel drum, in which he discovers he can create tunes by banging on discarded cans. Includes author's note, glossary, and sources"—Provided by publisher.

     ISBN 978-1-60060-652-6 (hardcover : alk. paper)

1. Simon, Winston, 1927-1976—Juvenile literature. 2. Musicians—Trinidad and Tobago—Biography—Juvenile literature. 3. Steel drum (Musical instrument)—Juvenile literature. I. Lessac, Frané, ill. II. Title.

ML3930.S552G74 2012   786.9'4092—dc23   [B]   2011045370